Strawberry Shortcake's
Berry Merry Christmas

adapted by Monique Z. Stephens

illustrated by Laura Thomas and Tom Ungrey

Grosset & Dunlap • New York

Strawberry Shortcake™ © 2003 Those Characters From Cleveland, Inc. Used under license by Penguin Group (USA) Inc. All rights reserved.
Published by Grosset & Dunlap, a division of Penguin Young Readers Group, 345 Hudson Street, New York, NY 10014. GROSSET & DUNLAP is a trademark
of Penguin Group (USA) Inc. Published simultaneously in Canada. Printed in USA. The scanning, uploading and distribution of this book via
the Internet or via any other means of the publisher is illegal and punishable by law. Please purchase only authorized electronic editions,
and do not participate or encourage electronic piracy of copyrighted materials. Your support of the author's rights is appreciated.

Library of Congress Cataloging-in-Publication Data is available.

ISBN 0-448-43200-5   A B C D E F G H I J

It was Christmastime in Strawberryland, Strawberry Shortcake's berry favorite time of year.

"Good job, Apple!" said Strawberry as her little sister, Apple Dumplin', reached up and placed a shining ornament on their Christmas tree. "While you're busy decorating the tree, I'll start making my shopping list.

"Let's see. I have to buy presents for Angel Cake, Orange Blossom, Ginger Snap, Huckleberry Pie, and Honey Pie Pony," Strawberry said as she wrote their names. "And I can't forget about you, Apple, or Custard and Pupcake!"

Just then, Strawberry Shortcake's friends arrived, carrying boxes of pretty ornaments and sparkly tinsel. They had come to help Strawberry decorate her Christmas tree.

"Hi everyone," said Strawberry. "Apple Dumplin' and I already started trimming the tree, but I'm afraid I have to go out. I still have Christmas shopping to do! Would you take care of Apple while I'm gone?"

"Sure! But will you have enough time to finish your shopping?" asked Ginger Snap. "Tomorrow's Christmas day, you know!"

"Can I go? Can I go?" Honey asked. "I know just where to take you, Strawberry!"

"That sounds great," said Strawberry. "With your help, I'll be finished in no time!" She put on her coat and scarf and climbed onto Honey's back. Then they set off down the road.

Soon they came to Holidayland,
a magical place full of Christmas spirit.
"Oh, it's so pretty!" Strawberry
cried, looking around in delight.
They walked into a store called
Sugar Plumdales.

A friendly-looking woman standing behind the counter greeted them.

"Hi! I'm the Sugar Plum Fairy. Can I help you?" she asked.

Strawberry Shortcake nodded. "Yes, please! I'm looking for a present for my friend Orange Blossom."

"Well, if you tell me about her, maybe I can help you find a gift she'll like," the Sugar Plum Fairy offered.

Honey walked over to an aisle full of saddles. "I'll tell you what she would like. She'd love one of these fabulous saddles!"

"Honey, Orange Blossom's not a horse, you know," said Strawberry. "She doesn't even ride horses! We need to get Orange something that *she* will like. And what *she* likes is planting and gardening—and fruit!"

"In that case, it sounds like sugarplums could be the right gift for Orange Blossom," said the Sugar Plum Fairy. She reached behind the counter and brought out a sugarplum bush.

"That's perfect!" Strawberry cried. "Thank you so much. How much do I owe you?"

"How about just giving me some of those juicy strawberries?" asked the Sugar Plum Fairy.

Strawberry smiled and handed her a basket of bright red berries.

Next they went to the Candy-cane Mart. Tiny gnomes were running around the room, frantically stacking candy canes. The red-and-white striped candies were everywhere— crowding the shelves, spilling out of baskets, and covering the floor in mountainous piles.

"Oh my goodness!" exclaimed Strawberry Shortcake. "What's going on here?"

"Something's happened to the Amazing Candy-cane Machine!" one of the gnomes answered. "We can't slow it down!" He pointed to a tall machine at the back of the room. It was spitting out dozens of candy canes every minute!

Strawberry Shortcake stood back and peered up at the controls. "I think I see the problem," she said. "But I'll need your help to fix it."

A group of gnomes formed a pyramid on Honey's back and Strawberry quickly climbed to the top. She turned the switch from *high* to *low*. The machine slowed down until it was at the perfect speed: every few minutes, one candy cane popped out.

Everyone cheered as Strawberry carefully climbed down to the floor.

One of the gnomes stepped forward. "How can we ever thank you for your help?" he asked.

"Well, I'm looking for a present for my friend Ginger Snap," said Strawberry.

"Got any saddles?" Honey asked.

"Oh, Honey!" said Strawberry. "A saddle wouldn't be right at all. But Ginger loves cookies."

"Perhaps your friend might like these," said the gnome. He pointed to a display of cookie cutters in fun Christmas shapes. Then he gave her a wagon piled with candy canes. "And some candy canes, of course!"

"This wagon is the perfect present for Apple Dumplin'!" said Strawberry as they left the Candy-cane Mart. Soon they entered a place called Holly Woods.

Angelic voices called out to them. "Merry Christmas! Merry Christmas!"

Strawberry looked up. "Listen! Angels on the treetops are talking to us!"

One of the tree angels greeted them. "Hello. What brings you to Holly Woods today?" she asked.

"I'm looking for Christmas presents for my friends," Strawberry answered. She checked her list. "Let's see... I still need presents for Angel Cake and Custard."

"I'll help you," said the tree angel. "Let's start with Custard. Tell me all about her."

"Well, she enjoys sleeping," said Strawberry.

"How about a sleeping willow tree?" the tree angel suggested. "Or an alarm clock tree?"

Strawberry shook her head. "I don't think so. A sleeping willow might make her want to sleep even more. And she gets upset when someone wakes her up. Did I mention that she's a cat?"

"A cat?" said the tree angel. "Why didn't you say so? She'll need a cat tree—something that is perfect for scratching. And for your friend Angel . . ."

She handed Strawberry a small angel figurine.

"Thank you berry much!" said Strawberry Shortcake.

Strawberry and Honey continued on to Carol Lane, a street filled with nutcrackers who were singing Christmas carols.

"If you're looking for a gift for Pupcake, I think a saddle would be an excellent choice," said Honey.

"Oh, Honey, what would a dog do with a saddle? How would you feel if Pupcake gave you a bone?" Strawberry asked.

"A bone?" said Honey. "That would be silly. What would a pony do with a bone?"

"Exactly!" replied Strawberry.

Honey started singing along with the carolers. "Jingle bells, jingle bells . . ."

"That's it!" Strawberry cried. "A collar with bells! Pupcake loves making noise. And that way, we would always know where he was."

Strawberry walked right into Carol Carroll's Bell Shoppe. The nice shopkeeper helped her pick out a collar with a shiny gold bell for Pupcake.

"Perfect!" said Strawberry happily.

"I still don't have a gift for Huckleberry Pie," Strawberry said sadly.

"Let's look in Holidayland's Northern Outskirts," Honey suggested. "I bet we'll find something there."

As they made their way to the Northern Outskirts, a strong, gusty wind whipped up around them. It started snowing.

Then the storm became even fiercer, blowing Strawberry and Honey from side to side.

"Hang on, Strawberry! Hang on!" Honey cried. She was swept off her feet as the blizzard carried them straight through the doors of a building!

Strawberry Shortcake looked around—and found herself face-to-face with Santa Claus! She gasped. "Oh my goodness! We're in Santa's Workshop!"

"Hello, Strawberry," said Santa kindly. "I hear you've been berry good. Now, what would you like for Christmas?"

"Um . . . I don't know. I don't really need anything for myself," said Strawberry. "But I do want to find a special present for my friend Huckleberry."

"I know just what I want, Santa," Honey said. "I want a new saddle, new reins, new spurs, new horseshoes, some carrots . . ."

"Whoa there, Honey," Santa laughed. "I know all about you. And I know all about you and your friends, too, Strawberry. You'll find a present that's just right for Huck. I promise."

As they left Santa's Workshop, Strawberry Shortcake and Honey saw two giggling elves having a snowball fight.

"I've never seen a snowball before," said Strawberry. "In Strawberryland it only snows berries!"

She bent down and quickly made a large snowball. She tossed it at Honey, who ducked just in time.

Strawberry giggled. "That's berry fun!" she said. "I wish Huckleberry Pie were here to have a snowball fight with us. I know! I'll give Huck snowballs for Christmas!"

"I still think a nice saddle is the way to go," said Honey. But she helped Strawberry roll snowballs for Huck anyway.

It was dark when Strawberry Shortcake and Honey finally reached Strawberry's cottage.

"I can't wait to give everyone their presents—especially Huck," Strawberry said happily. But when she went to unhitch the wagon, she cried out in surprise.

"Oh, no! Huck's snowballs—they've melted!" Even worse, the melted snowballs had ruined all the other gifts, too—including Apple's wagon, which had started to rust.

A tear rolled down Strawberry's cheek. There was no time to get new gifts for everyone. She went inside to tell her friends what had happened, but they were all fast asleep.

On Christmas morning, everyone woke up happy and excited—everyone except Strawberry Shortcake. "I'm sorry, everybody," she said sadly. "I don't have presents for any of you!" She explained what had happened to their gifts.

Huck put his arm around her shoulder. "It doesn't matter to us, Strawberry. Christmas is about friendship and love, not about presents."

Her friends nodded in agreement. Strawberry smiled in relief.

Suddenly, Orange Blossom laughed. "Hey, Strawberry, what's with the big joke? If our gifts were ruined, what are all these presents?" She pointed at the Christmas tree. Underneath were several beautifully wrapped gifts.

Strawberry looked on in amazement as everyone opened their gifts. Each one of her friends had just the present she'd picked out for them. There was even a pile of snowballs for Huck!

"Where did all these presents come from?" Strawberry wondered. Suddenly, she remembered Santa Claus's promise—that everything would turn out just right.

Pupcake picked up an oddly shaped present and trotted over to Honey.

Honey tore into the wrapping. "For me? A present? A—bone?!" she sputtered. "A bone for a pony?"

"Honey, now do you see what I mean about getting someone a gift they will really like?" Strawberry asked gently.

Honey hung her head. "You're right. I get it now."

Strawberry picked up another gift from under the tree and handed it to Honey. The pony opened it and cheered. "A brand new saddle! It's just what I wanted! Thank you so much!"